PADDY
and the

Magic Pirate Hat

Written by Jenny Album   Illustrated by Claire Keay

little boo publishing

For Uncle Alfy.

Special thanks to Katie Shmuel

Published in 2016 by Little Boo Publishing

ISBN: 978-0-9934203-5-1

Also by this author:

little boo publishing

A pirate came to Paddy's birthday party this year.

He was named 'Pirate Jim'
and he did games, magic tricks,
and pin the tail on the donkey with
really great prizes!

After the party, Paddy saw
Pirate Jim getting ready to leave.
He looked a little different now.
He was wearing sneakers and a wool hat with a pom-pom.

"Why have you taken
off all your pirate clothes?"
asked Paddy.
"Does that mean that you
are not a real pirate?
Or even a real magician?"

"Of course I'm a real pirate!"
said Pirate Jim.

"And I'm a real
magician too.
But I put on ordinary
clothes as a disguise...
so nobody can tell that
I'm actually a pirate."

"In fact," Pirate Jim continued, "I am not just a pirate, I'm a *Magic Pirate King*. My great great grandfather Pirate Flaharty M'Hearty was the most famous Magic Pirate King of all.

"He had a special magic pirate hat that helped him find hidden treasure."

"But in the end he gave all his treasure away!"
"Why did he do that?" asked Paddy.

"He said that 'real treasure' was actually *nothing* to do with the things that are kept in a treasure chest," replied Pirate Jim.

"And after that, he only went on treasure hunts if it was to help people find important things that they had lost."

"Wow," said Paddy. "I would like to become a Magic Pirate King!"

"Well," said Pirate Jim, "I'm afraid you can't. Not unless you too can discover what *real* treasure is."

"But I already know what real treasure is!" said Paddy. "It's gold and jewels, and valuable gems like diamonds and rubies!"

"Really?" said Pirate Jim. "So would you say that *plastic* is treasure then, Paddy?"

"No, of course not," Paddy replied.

"How about glass?" asked Pirate Jim.

"Er, not really, no." Paddy replied.

"And paper?" asked Pirate Jim.

"Now you're just being silly!" said Paddy.

"Well," said Pirate Jim, "I'm sorry to say that you are just not ready to become a Magic Pirate King."

"Oh," said Paddy sadly. "Well, how do I become ready?"

"I'll tell you what," said Pirate Jim,
"take this *magic pirate hat*, and perhaps you'll find out one day."

"Now," said Pirate Jim. "If ever you need to go on a really *important* treasure hunt, you must do two things – first, put this hat on, and then, look around for a 'message in a bottle'..."

With that, Pirate Jim wandered out of the door and onto the bus.

The next day, Paddy found
his mother looking a little upset.
"Oh dear, Paddy, I seem to have
lost something very precious
to me," she said.

"It's a plastic toy ring that my friend Emily gave
me when I was a little girl."

"I was feeling sad, and she wanted to cheer me up.
From that day on, Emily and I became best friends.
And we still are today!

"I've kept
that ring safe
all these years,
but your sister
was playing
with it, and
now it's
disappeared!

"It might just be a plastic toy, but it means more to me than the
precious grown up jewellery I wear now."

Paddy put on his pirate hat.
He figured it must be time
for a 'treasure hunt'!

He looked all over for a 'message in a bottle'...

Finally, in
the bathroom
he noticed a
bottle of
pink bubble
bath - with
a note inside.

The note said:

You must face some mighty waves,
Then *seek* some *sandy shores*.

Then dig down deep, and you will find
The thing that is adored...

"Hmm... 'sandy shores', eh?"
thought Paddy - and he walked
towards the sandbox...

Unfortunately, thanks to his sister,
he did indeed have to brave some pretty 'mighty waves'!

When he got to the sandbox he started digging.
He dug and dug and dug.

He found a
plastic ball, an old doll's
hat, and a bottle top.

Suddenly, he saw
something shimmering in
the sun... and guess what?

It was Paddy's
mom's special
plastic ring!

When his mother saw it she was so happy!

"My ring! Thank you so much Paddy," she said.

"Or should I say *Pirate Paddy*?"

The next day, Paddy noticed his next door neighbour,
Mrs Glennon looked a bit sad. She said: "My son lives far away in
Australia, and he's just had his first baby. He has sent me some
photos of her.

"But I can't find my glasses, and without them I can't see
the photos at all!"

Paddy put on his magic pirate hat – he figured it was time for another treasure hunt!

Deep in the kitchen recycling can, he saw an old ketchup bottle with a rolled up note inside.

This is what the note said:

Look for an ancient wooden shack,
If you want to bring your treasure back.

You must be strong and bold,
Seek something that gleams like
coins of gold...

Paddy went into
Mrs Glennon's back yard to look
for an 'ancient wooden shack'.

He spotted an old looking
garden shed.
He went inside.

"Hmm... gold coins,
gold coins...?"
pondered Paddy,
as he looked around.

He picked up an upside
down flower pot, but underneath
were only a few surprised bugs!

Next he saw some brown
bags in the corner.

"Ah.. bags full of pirate
booty!" thought Paddy.

But there was only
brown soil inside...

Then Paddy looked up at the wall of the shed. On it were hundreds of gleaming little circles of light!

"Wow!" thought Paddy. "They look just like gold coins! But how did they get there?" he wondered.

On the window sill
he saw a pair of glasses.

Sunlight was gleaming through them,
making the little round discs of light appear on the wall.

Paddy took the glasses over to
Mrs Glennon and she was so pleased!

"Now I will finally be
able to see what my baby
granddaughter looks like!
Thank you so much
Paddy – or should I say
Pirate Paddy!"

A bit later on, Paddy noticed his dad looking a bit grumpy.
"Paddy, I seem to have lost something that means a great
deal to me..." he said.

"Dad – I bet you I can find it!
In fact, you don't even have to tell me what it is!" said Paddy.

Paddy put on his magic pirate hat.

In his mom's bedroom he found a perfume bottle with a note inside.

The note said:

In a place full of tropical flowers,
Lies something as heavy as a boulder.

You must push this thing aside,
Perhaps by using your shoulder...

The treasure you seek is a very old scroll,
On which 'X' does mark the spot.

It may not seem like treasure to you,
But to someone it means a lot...

Paddy ran into the living room.

Here, there was a
very heavy couch
covered in flowers!

He pushed the couch, (using his shoulder, as the note had said).

But he accidently
knocked over a china vase.

Paddy's dad heard the crash and came running in.

"Oh no, look what you've done, Paddy! That's your mom's vase. She'll be so upset.

"You really should be more careful! I'm not happy with you at all. Now go up to your room."

Sadly, Paddy made
his way to his bedroom.

"Oh dear," he thought,
"I was only trying to help,
but now I've broken
mom's vase.
I'll probably
be in so much
trouble now."

After a while Paddy's dad knocked on the door, smiling.
"Hey Paddy, guess what?" he said. "It turns out
that your mother never really liked
that vase, so she doesn't mind
that it broke.

"And, you know what else? I've found the special thing that I lost.
It was tucked inside the broken vase! Your sister must have put it there."

Paddy's dad had been holding a rolled up piece of paper.

It was a drawing of Paddy and his dad, that Paddy had drawn for him one Father's Day.

On the picture Paddy had written:
"To the best Dad in the world, love Paddy".
He had added a big 'X', and lots of smaller kisses too!

Paddy's dad said, "I love this so much Paddy!"

"I wouldn't swap this old piece of paper for all the gold and jewels in the world!

"Thanks Pirate Paddy!"

A few days later, Paddy spotted Pirate Jim
in the supermarket!

Paddy said,
"Pirate Jim – you
know what you
were saying
before
about 'glass',
'plastic' and
'paper' being
treasure and
everything...?

"Well, I didn't
understand what
you meant then,
but I think I do
now!"

"Well done Paddy," said Pirate Jim.
"I knew you had what it took to be a Magic Pirate King!"

Then Pirate Jim handed a box of laundry detergent to Paddy's mom.

"I think you forgot something, Mrs Kearney..."

Then he waved goodbye and wandered down the frozen vegetable aisle.

"How on earth did he know I had forgotten my laundry detergent?" muttered Paddy's mom.

When Paddy's mom got home she found a bag of chocolate coins hidden inside the box.

"I can't understand how these got in here - this box was sealed shut!" she said.

"Oh well, I guess you might as well have them, Paddy. After all, you've been a good boy and helped lots of people this week."

Paddy took his chocolate coins up to his room,
and thought about the last few days.

"Hmm... I think
Pirate Jim was right.
The really 'special' things,
the things that really count
as *treasure*, are not just
jewels, gold and silver, but
the things that make you
feel happy deep inside."

"But you know what...?"
he thought with a smile,
"Chocolate coins are *pretty special* too!"

Made in the USA
Middletown, DE
06 October 2017